The
Biggest Star

JERYN ALISE TURNER

HIGGINS PUBLISHING
DALLAS, TEXAS

Library of Congress Control Number: 2022916417
Pages cm. 34

Higgins Publishing
The Biggest Star / Turner, Jeryn Alise

ISBN: 978-1-941580-50-9 (HB) * 978-1-941580-40-0 (PB) * 978-1-941580-31-8 (EB)

1. (JUV039030) JUVENILE FICTION / Social Themes / Death, Grief, Bereavement
2. (JUV030050) JUVENILE FICTION / Social Themes / Emotions & Feelings
3. (JUV013000) JUVENILE FICTION / Family / General

For information about special discounts for bulk purchases, subsidiary, foreign and translations rights contact Higgins Publishing at contact@higginspublishing.com.

The unthinkable teaches you to seek understanding. I wrote this book to honor the beautiful souls whose love continues to live through me. I hear your words often and carry you in my heart. I dedicate this book to children dealing with loss, may this book comfort your spirit.

In loving memory of Nikki Scales

I'm sorry
I didn't say goodbye
to my favorite
little girl and guy.

I know you are sad
and it's okay to cry.
It's normal to miss me
and wonder why.

Talk things out,
don't hold in your feelings.
Focus more on our memories
than my leaving.

Look at pictures,
it's okay to say my name.
Although different,
I still love you the same.

Being with you
gave me so much joy!
Continue to live
the life we enjoyed.

Go to the places
you and I loved to see.
While there,
you'll fondly remember me.

I'll always be with you
wherever you go
Constantly watching over you
as you grow.

14

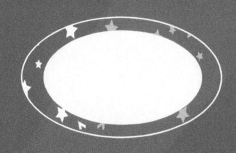

Until we meet again,
I'll stay by your side;
Sending messages,
acting as your guide.

Butterflies and rainbows
are beautiful signs;
Letting you know
that everything is fine.

18

As your Guardian Angel,
I will always be here.
You are not alone,
you have nothing to fear.

Don't be angry at God,
continue to pray.
I'm with Him in Heaven,
I hear what you say.

Words are powerful
as long as you believe.
Whatever you ask for,
you will receive.

So before you
go to sleep at night,
find The Biggest Star;
that's my spirit shining bright.

Hold on to the love
I placed in your heart;
For when you do,
we will never be apart.

I will always be with you!

Grief Gifts For Children

SCAN TO BUY BLANKET

SCAN TO BUY COMFORTER

SCAN TO BUY PILLOW

Thank you so much for your purchase!

If you enjoyed this book, please post a review on the site where you purchased this book.

AMAZON
SCAN TO REVIEW

SCAN TO BUY

What Do You See?

JERYN ALISE TURNER

Lightning Source UK Ltd.
Milton Keynes UK
UKHW050230011122
411431UK00002B/2